MAR 14 2018

ELK GROVE VILLAGE PUBLIC LIBRARY
3 1250 01206 7900

18

W9-BRF-657

DISCARDED
Elk Grove Village
Public Library

ELK GROVE VILLAGE PUBLIC LIBRARY
1001 WELLINGTON AVE.
ELK GROVE VILLAGE, IL 60007
(847) 439-0447

# THE WEATHER GIRLS

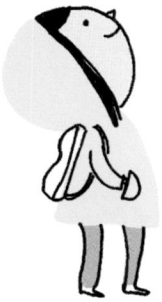

TO SEBASTIAN, MY DREAM CATCHER . . .

Henry Holt and Company
New York

Laura
Miffy
Annie
Rebecca
Jane
Vanessa
June
Melanie

MEET THE
WEATHER
GIRLS
Sarah
Cathleen
Lucy
Zoe
Kirsten
Tilly
Joy
Emily

It's summertime. We rise and shine!
All set to go, we form a line.

A big, bright sun.

Let's have some fun!

We swim and dive and splash and run.

Lush green forest, fresh clean air.
Look at all the creatures there!

Fall is windy in the city.
Trees are gold and red and pretty.

It's time for sweaters and for fun.

Through fallen leaves

we run and run!

We hop on bikes and ride and ride.

We pick apples

side by side.

Wintertime brings lots of snow.

*Brrrr, brrrr*, girls.

Let's go, go, go!

Through a blizzard, climb
and
climb.

The mountain's tall.

It takes some time.

The snow has stopped,

and we do, too.

The sky is big
and bright
and blue.

Spring is springing
through the trees.

We can feel the gentle breeze.

A big balloon!

Hooray,
hooray!

Up we go; we float away.

Strong winds blow. . . .

We fly, fly, fly.

Now look up—

a rainbow sky.

# MEET THE SEASONS

## WINTER, SPRING, SUMMER, FALL—THE WEATHER GIRLS LOVE THEM ALL!

## SUMMER

We see lots of animals out and about.
Plants are greenest. Temperatures are highest.
Days are longest. Sunshine is strongest.

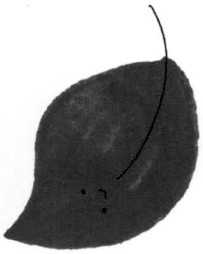

## FALL

We see fewer animals. Leaves change colors
and fall from the trees. Temperatures are cooler.
Days get shorter. There's less sunshine.

## WINTER

Many animals hibernate or travel for warmer weather. Some trees and plants are bare of leaves. Temperatures are coldest. Days are shortest. Sunshine is weakest.

## SPRING

We start to see more animals. Trees and plants grow new leaves and become greener. Flowers bloom. Temperatures are rising. Days get longer. There's more sunshine.

Henry Holt and Company
*Publishers since 1866*
Henry Holt® is a registered trademark of Macmillan Publishing Group, LLC
175 Fifth Avenue, New York, New York 10010
mackids.com

Copyright © 2018 by Aki
All rights reserved.

Library of Congress Cataloging-in-Publication Data is available.
ISBN 978-1-62779-620-0

Our books may be purchased in bulk for promotional, educational, or business use.
Please contact your local bookseller or the Macmillan Corporate and Premium
Sales Department at (800) 221-7945 ext. 5442 or by e-mail at MacmillanSpecialMarkets@macmillan.com.

First edition, 2018 / Designed by April Ward
Printed in China by RR Donnelley Asia Printing Solutions Ltd., Dongguan City, Guangdong Province

1 3 5 7 9 10 8 6 4 2